Where is Igglepiggle's blanket?

Andrew Davenport

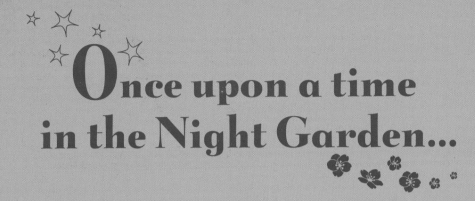

Once upon a time in the Night Garden...

Igglepiggle came to play.

Yes, my name is Igglepiggle,
Iggle-piggle-wiggle-niggle-diggle!
Yes, my name is Igglepiggle,
Iggle-piggle-wiggle-niggle-noo!

Igglepiggle has a favourite thing.
Do you know what it is?

It's Igglepiggle's blanket.

One day, Igglepiggle
lost his blanket.
Has anybody seen
Igglepiggle's blanket?

Tombliboo!

The Tombliboos hadn't seen
Igglepiggle's blanket.

Don't worry, Igglepiggle.
We'll find your blanket.

Brring-brring!
The trubliphone is ringing.

Who is calling on the trubliphone?

Mi-mi-mi-mi-mi-mi-mi!

Said a teeny tiny voice.

Igglepiggle didn't know
who it was.

Has anybody seen
Igglepiggle's blanket?

Upsy Daisy!

Upsy Daisy hadn't seen
Igglepiggle's blanket.

Don't worry, Igglepiggle.
We'll find your blanket.

Brring-brring!
The trubliphone
is ringing again.

Who is calling on the
trubliphone?

Mi-mi-mi!

Mi-mi-mi-mi-mi-mi-mi!

Mi-mi-mi-mi-mi!

Said lots of teeny tiny voices.

Igglepiggle still didn't know who it was.

Has anybody seen Igglepiggle's blanket?

Makka Pakka!

Makka Pakka hadn't seen Igglepiggle's blanket.

Mi-mi-mi-mi-mi-mi-mi!

Who is that calling, Igglepiggle?

Look at that.
It's Igglepiggle's blanket!

Mi-mi-mi-mi-mi-mi-mi-mi-mi!

Said Igglepiggle's blanket.

Igglepiggle's blanket
doesn't usually say
Mi-mi-mi-mi-mi-mi-mi-mi-mi!

Igglepiggle picked up his blanket.
There was something underneath...

The teeny, tiny Pontipines!
So that's who was calling on the trubliphone!

Igglepiggle's blanket was on top of
the Pontipine's house!

Isn't that a pip?

Once upon a time
in the Night Garden,
Igglepiggle lost his blanket.

Brrrring-brrrrring!
The trubliphone rang.

Mi-mi-mi-mi-mi-mi-mi!

Who is calling on
the trubliphone?

There is your blanket
Igglepiggle!

And there are
the Pontipines!

Thank you, Pontipines.

Time to go to sleep everybody.

Go to sleep, Pontipines.

Go to sleep, Upsy Daisy.

Go to sleep, Makka Pakka.

Go to sleep, Tombliboos.

Go to sleep, Haahoos.

Go to sleep Ninky Nonk
and go to sleep, Pinky Ponk.

Wait a minute.
Somebody is not in bed!
Who's not in bed?
Igglepiggle is not in bed!

Don't worry, Igglepiggle...
it's time to go.